Help me, Herman.

Herman the Helper

BY ROBERT KRAUS

PICTURES BY
JOSE ARUEGO & ARIANE DEWEY

Simon and Schuster Books for Young Readers
Published by Simon & Schuster Inc., New York

Don't worry, I'll help you.

Text copyright © 1974 by Robert Kraus
Illustrations copyright © 1974 by Jose Aruego and Ariane Dewey
All rights reserved
including the right of reproduction
in whole or in part in any form.
Published by Simon and Schuster Books for Young Readers
A Division of Simon & Schuster, Inc.
Simon & Schuster Building
Rockefeller Center
1230 Avenue of the Americas
New York, NY 10020

10 9 8 7 6 5 4 3 2

10 9 8 7 6 5   pbk

Simon and Schuster Books for Young Readers
is a trademark of Simon & Schuster, Inc.
Originally published by Windmill Books, Inc.
Manufactured in the United States of America

Library of Congress Cataloging-in-Publication Data
Kraus, Robert, 1925–
    Herman the helper/by Robert Kraus; pictures by Jose Aruego & Ariane Dewey.
p.   cm.
Reprint. Originally published: New York: Windmill Books, 1974.
Summary: Herman the helpful octopus is always willing to assist
anyone who needs his help—old or young, friend or enemy.
ISBN 0-671-66270-8pbk   0-671-66887-0
[1. Octopus—Fiction. 2. Brotherliness—Fiction. 3. Helpfulness—
Fiction.]   I. Aruego, Jose, ill. II. Dewey, Ariane, ill.
III. Title.
[PZ7.K868HF 1987] 87-32071
[E]—dc 19 CIP AC

For Pamela, Bruce, Billy & Juan

Herman liked to help.

Thank you, Herman.

He helped his mother.

That's nice, Herman.

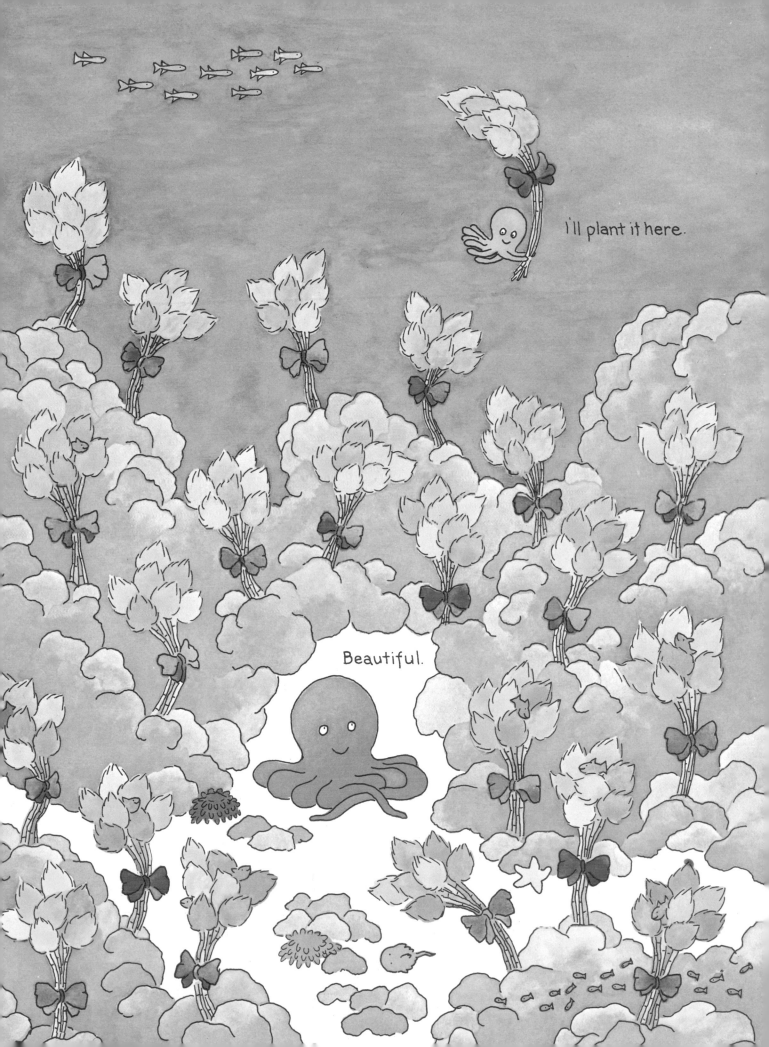

He helped his father.

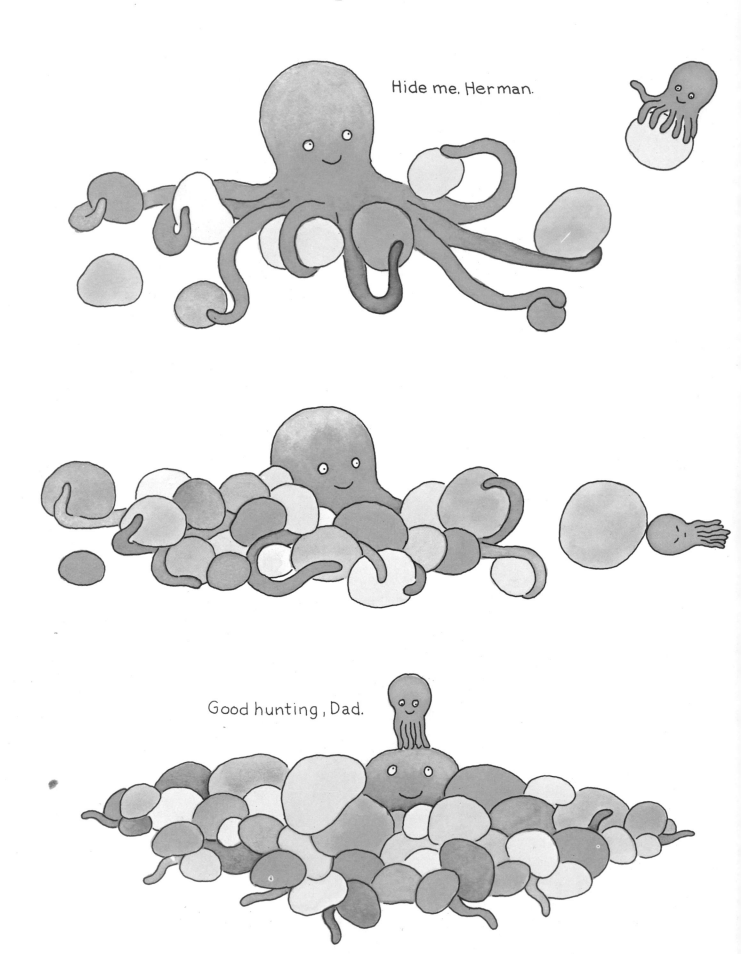

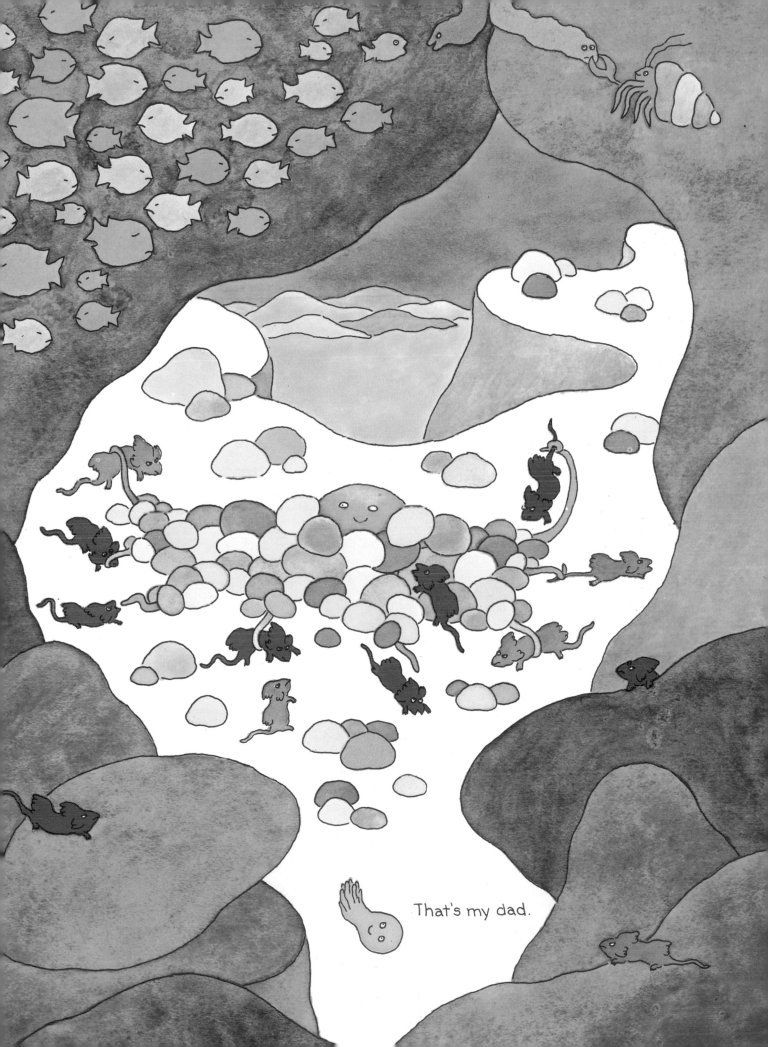

That's my dad.

He helped his brothers and sisters.

Thank you, brother.

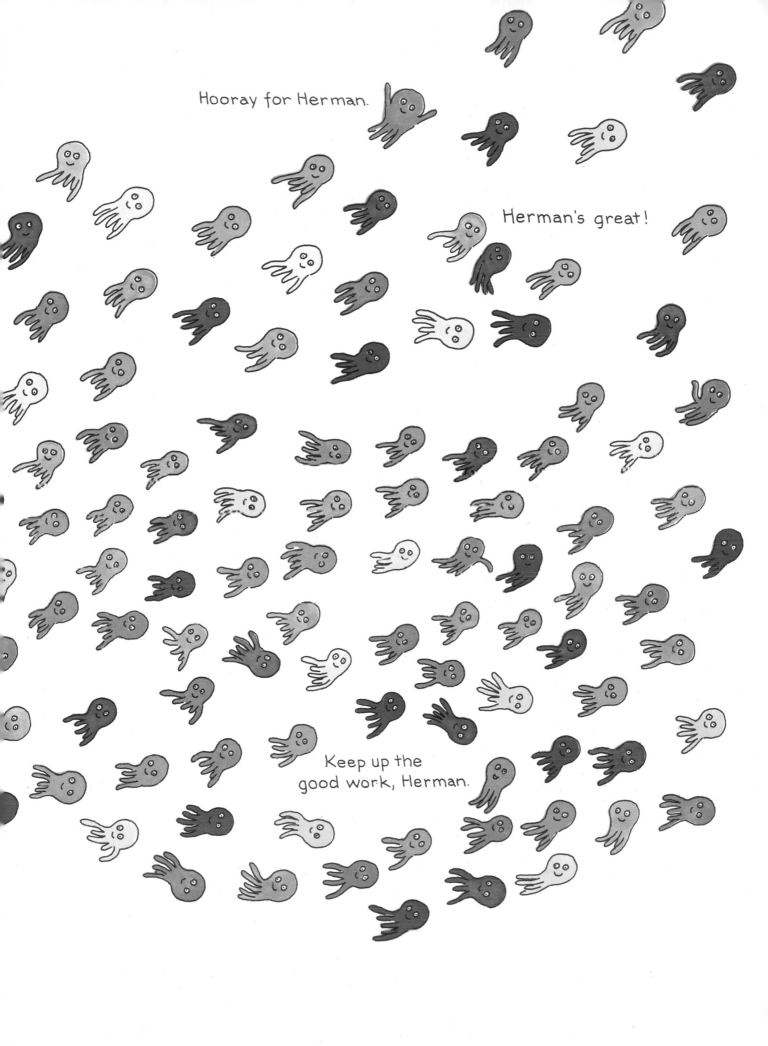

He helped his aunt.

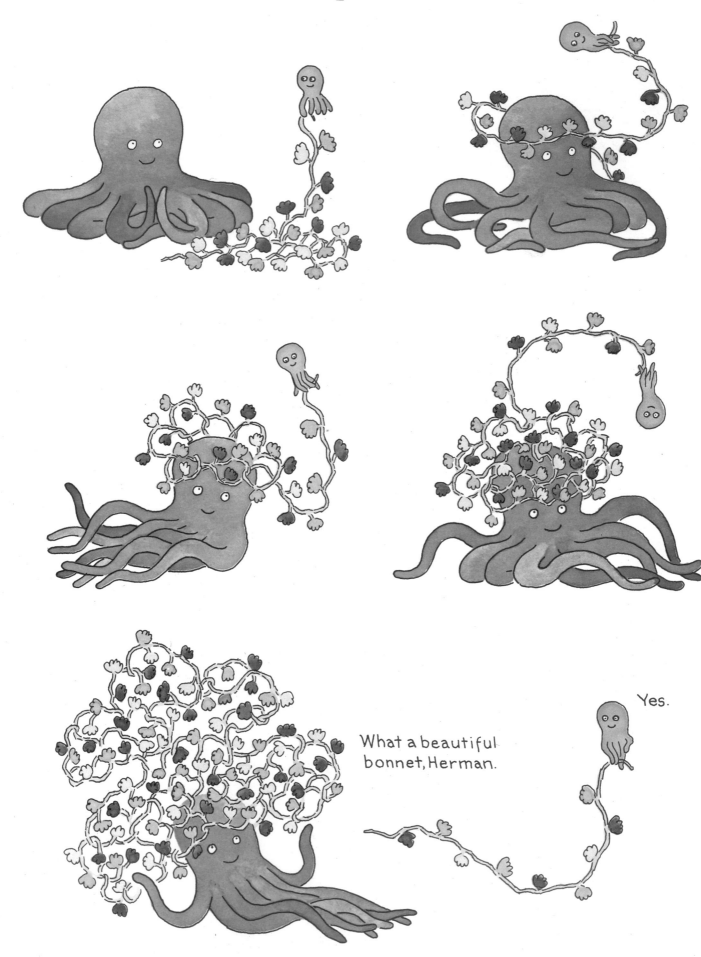

What a beautiful bonnet, Herman.

Yes.

He helped his uncle.

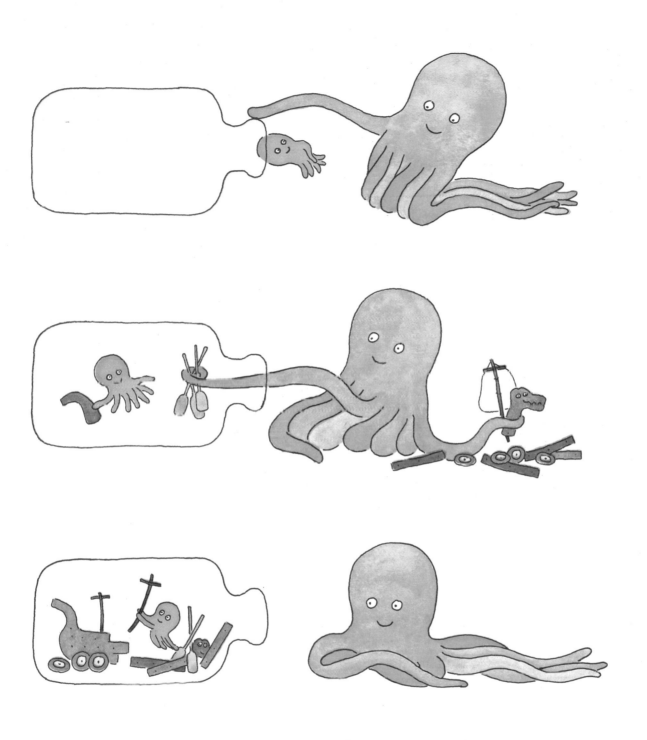

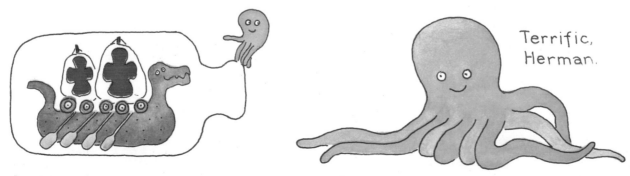

He helped his friends.

OOF!

UGH!

ICK!

URK!

OUCH!

Take it easy, Herman.

Many thanks, Herman.

He helped his enemies.

Okay.

Help! It's after us!

I'll camouflage you with my ink.

He helped the young.

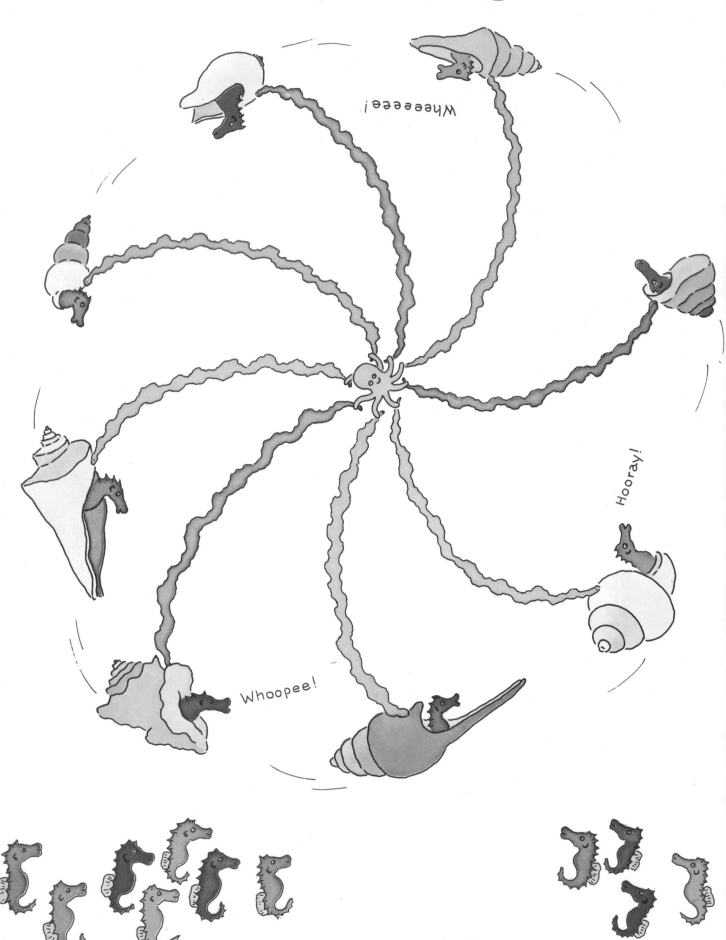

He helped the old.

Whoops!

This will help you swim.

He helped the poor and needy.

Our home is beautiful now.

Thanks to Herman.

He helped the fireman.

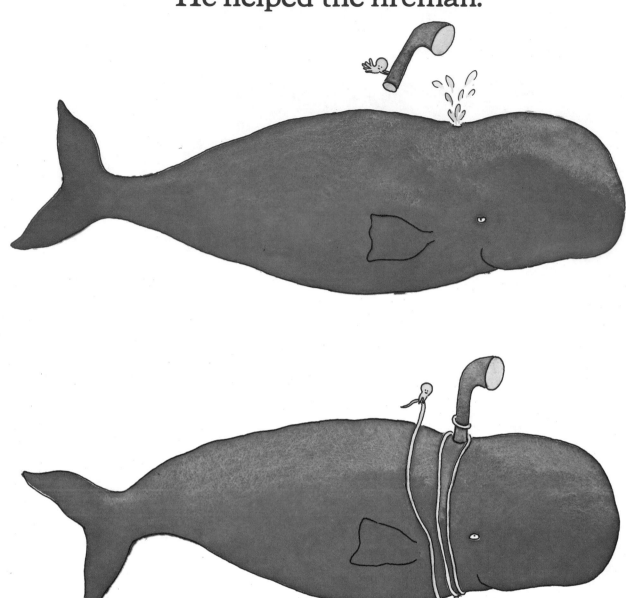

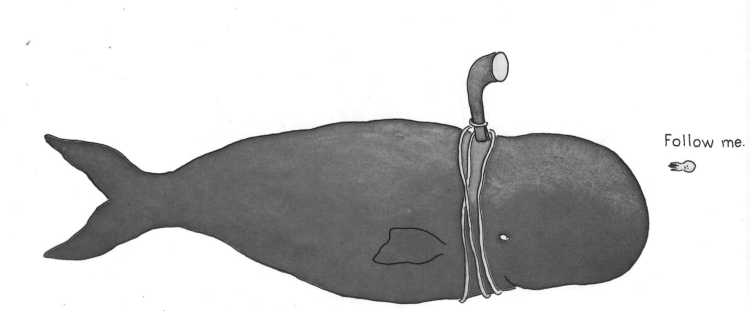

Follow me.

He helped the policeman.

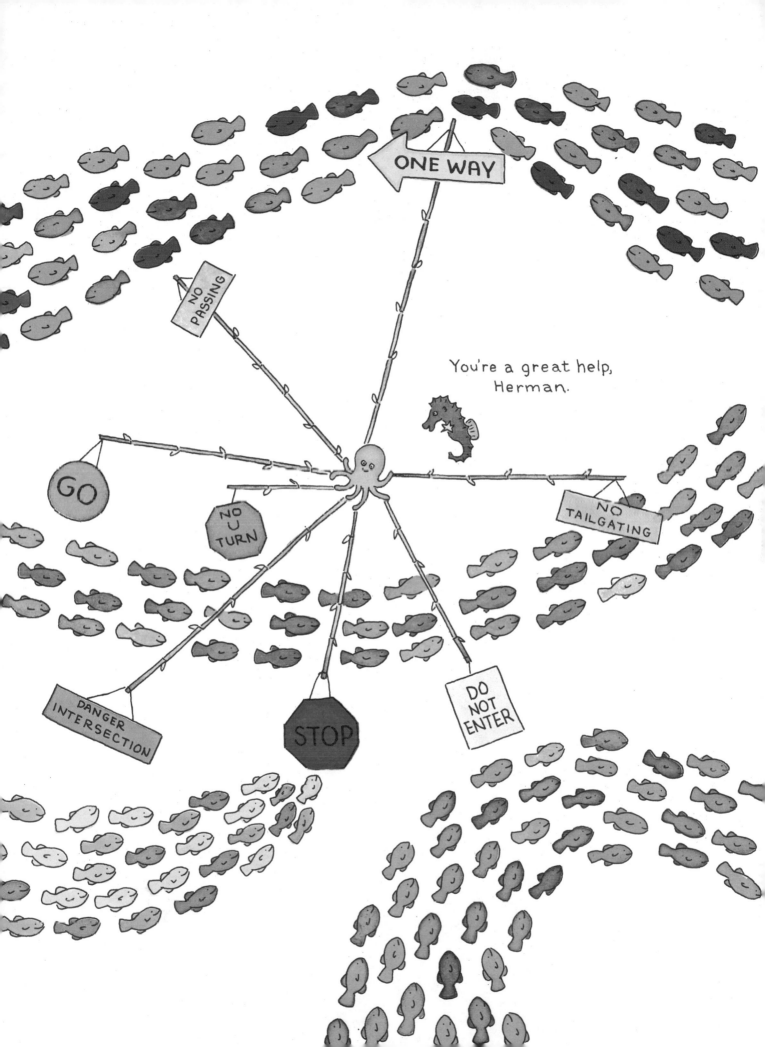

Then the clock struck six and Herman hurried home.

Six o'clock already?

He washed his hands and face.

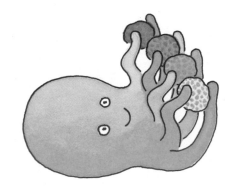

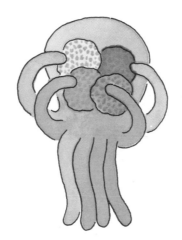

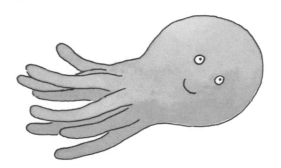

I'm hungry!

And sat down to supper.

"May I help you to some mashed potatoes?" asked Herman's father.

"No thanks,"
said Herman,
"I'll help myself."

Thank you,
Herman.